To: Saoirse

From: Grandma Sandy

How to Catch Santa Claus

From the New York Times Bestselling Series by
Alice Walstead &
Andy Elkerton

sourcebooks
wonderland

'Twas the night before **CHRISTMAS**,
and all through the house,
the children have set traps—
and not for a mouse.

This makes sense to me.
Yes, I understand why!
I'm a holiday legend
with reindeer that fly.

As much as I want to stay for a while,
I have stops 'round the world tonight.
I'd love to talk to each child there is,
but these toys need homes by **daylight**.

To do.....

You're all so smart and clever,
and the traps do look like fun,
but I can't get too **distracted**.
There's a lot of work to be done!

I love Christmas flowers.
They grow at the NORTH POLE.
But I don't need to take these.
It's time for me to roll!

The tree looks so festive
and cozy in this nook.
The room is all decked out,
but an odd place to put a book.

FOR
YOU

Hope the presents bring joy.
I've added gifts to each list
because surprises are **important**.
I call it my gift-checklist-twist!

I bet no one knows about
the MAGIC KEY that I don't show.
I can walk from house to house,
to come in and then to go.

The trap fooled the **reindeer**,
and Elf, you don't get to smirk.
Other plots sure snagged you.
I hope kids don't know this works!

We've got to keep moving,
but I will pause for a snack.
Can't sit in the chair, though.
There's a toy sack to **UNPACK**!

SANTA
CATCHER
5000

Those **COOKIES** were good,
and no traps did I spy.
Time to call the sleigh team.
We're almost ready to fly!

Oh my, this is **IMPRESSIVE**.
It must have taken hours!
(But if I'm being honest,
I prefer the trap of flowers.)

ENTER HERE

There's one thing that's true:
these toys go under the tree.
I just can't see how to do that,
so I'm **sending** you and not me!

How did we get out you ask?
It looked like we were done for.
Santa's magic is very real,
and I cannot reveal more.

I've loved this visit
but I'm done here tonight
I'll be back next year,
time to fly out of sight.

Merry Christmas to all,
and to all a good night!

The art was first sketched, then painted digitally with brushes designed by the artist.

Published by Sourcebooks Wonderland, an imprint of Sourcebooks Kids
P.O. Box 4410, Naperville, Illinois 60567–4410
(630) 961-3900
sourcebookskids.com

Cataloging-in-Publication Data is on file with the Library of Congress.
Source of Production: Wing King Tong Paper Products Co. Ltd., Shenzhen, Guangdong Province, China
Date of Production: March 2023
Run Number: 5029736

Printed and bound in China.
WKT 10 9 8 7 6 5 4 3 2 1